Ethel's NEW *HOME*

by Kathy Rogo

illustrated by Natalia Starikova

To my **WONDERFUL** sons Kevin and JJ and my sweet little **HAMSTER ETHEL** whose escapades inspired my story.

	DATE DUE	10/16	

Ethel's NEW *HOME*

Ethel the dwarf hamster lived in a big glass tank on top of a big dresser next to a wall with her seven brothers and sisters. Their names were Lucy, Thelma, Fred, Elvis, Louise, Ricky and Sadie. They belonged to a young boy named Kevin and his little brother Timmy who would feed them every morning before they left for school.

1

One morning after Ethel woke up and stretched, she thought to herself, "I think I'll go for a run in the wheel before breakfast." But when Ethel got to the wheel, her sister Lucy was already running in it.

"I just got here!" exclaimed Lucy, huffing and puffing. "I'm sorry, you'll have to wait!"

"Okay," said Ethel. "I guess I'll just have breakfast."

But when Ethel got to the food dish, there was Fred and Ricky! There was not enough room for Ethel to eat out of the food dish, too.

"We just got here," they said. "We're sorry, you'll have to wait."

3

"Well, I am thirsty," thought Ethel. "I'll get a drink of water while I wait."

But when she got to the water bottle, there was Thelma.

"I just got here!" cried Thelma. "I'm sorry, you'll have to wait."

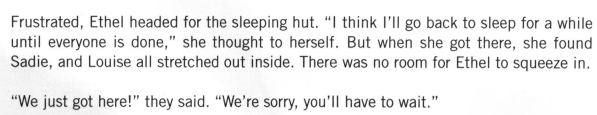

Frustrated, Ethel headed for the sleeping hut. "I think I'll go back to sleep for a while until everyone is done," she thought to herself. But when she got there, she found Sadie, and Louise all stretched out inside. There was no room for Ethel to squeeze in.

"We just got here!" they said. "We're sorry, you'll have to wait."

"I'm waiting too!" said Elvis, who was hanging from the ramp leading up to the hut. "We can share!"

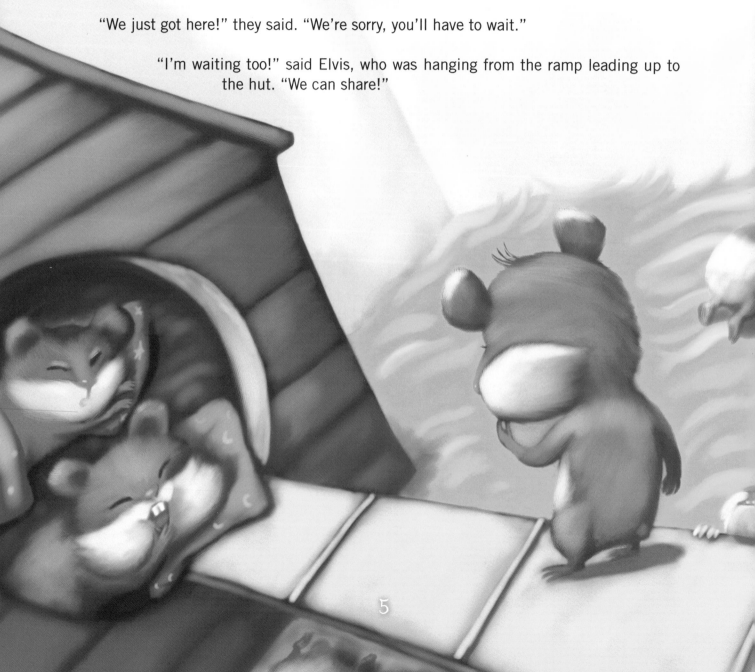

"I'm tired of having to wait all the time!" said Ethel, stamping her foot. "And I'm tired of sharing! I'm going to run away and find a place of my own!"

"What do you mean, Ethel?" asked Sadie, now wide-awake.

"I'm getting out of this hamster tank and finding a home of my own where I don't have to wait to run on the wheel, wait to have breakfast, wait to get a drink of water or even wait to take a nap. I'll be able to do whatever I want, whenever I want!" Ethel said excitedly.

"Oh really! And just how do you think you're going to get out of here?" asked Louise.

Ethel looked up at the top of the tank, then looked at the water bottle and thought for a minute.

"That's how I'll get out!" she exclaimed. "I better start packing!"

Ethel ran back to the food dish and pushed Fred and Ricky out of the way. She started packing her cheeks with food. Her cheeks got bigger and bigger as Sadie and Louise watched.

"Please don't leave Ethel," Louise wailed. "You don't know what's out there. Remember the big cat that looks at us through the glass? She's probably out there somewhere and wants to have you for a snack!"

"I'm not afraid of that old cat," said Ethel through her food-stuffed mouth. "Don't worry about me, I'll be just fine. And besides, I'm already packed and ready to go!"

7

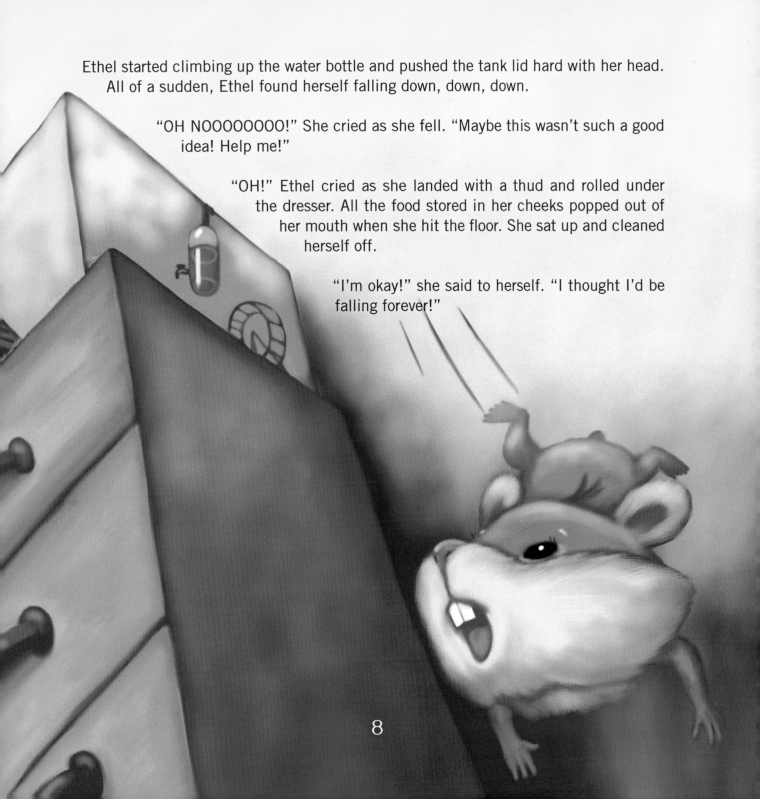

Ethel started climbing up the water bottle and pushed the tank lid hard with her head. All of a sudden, Ethel found herself falling down, down, down.

"OH NOOOOOOOO!" She cried as she fell. "Maybe this wasn't such a good idea! Help me!"

"OH!" Ethel cried as she landed with a thud and rolled under the dresser. All the food stored in her cheeks popped out of her mouth when she hit the floor. She sat up and cleaned herself off.

"I'm okay!" she said to herself. "I thought I'd be falling forever!"

8

Ethel started to re-pack her cheeks when she heard quiet humming.

"Who's there?" she asked nervously. A spider came crawling out of a shadowy corner straight at her!

"Oh my!" Ethel exclaimed, dropping her food again.

The spider was getting closer.

"How do I get out of here? Maybe this wasn't such a good idea!" Ethel said as she looked behind her and saw a light coming from the other side of the dresser.

"There's the way out!" she thought as she scurried toward the light and out into a big room.

"I know this place," she said to herself. "I'm still in the boy's room!"

9

Ethel looked back at the dresser; the spider was gone. Then she looked up and saw her brothers and sisters high up on the dresser, they looked so far away. Sadie, Louise, and Elvis watched anxiously. Ethel started to get a little scared.

"How am I going to get back home?" she cried.

Then Ethel saw the door. She forgot about being scared, forgot about her brothers and sisters and became very curious.

"Maybe if I go out there I will find a great new place to live," said Ethel. "I am going to be brave and see what is beyond that door."

10

Ethel scurried through the open doorway and stopped in a very big hallway.

"WOW!" she cried as she looked around.

The hallway was very bright and big, and at the end of it was another door. It was partly open, allowing sunshine to stream into the hallway where she was standing.

"There's my new home," Ethel said excitedly. "I will live in there!"

Ethel scurried down the hallway to the door. Once inside, she stopped and looked around. The room was very big, with a sofa at one end near the door. There was a big bed, nightstand, and a dresser at the other end. The sun was shining very brightly through a window somewhere above her head.

Ethel scurried under the bed and looked around.

"Too much room," she said. She came out from underneath the bed and scurried under the dresser "I could live under this dresser just fine," she decided. "I think I'll explore some more."

As Ethel came out from under the dresser, she heard a noise coming from the window and looked up.

Up on the windowsill stretching was the cat Louise had warned her about. "Oh dear, I think I am afraid of that old cat after all," Ethel thought to herself. "Maybe this wasn't such a good idea."

Ethel slowly started heading back the way she came. "I hope the cat doesn't see me," she whispered to herself.

Just then, the cat turned her big head and looked right at Ethel.

"Uh oh," Ethel cried. "Now what do I do?"

"What are you doing in here?" asked the cat, staring at Ethel with her big green eyes. "It's dangerous for a little hamster like you to be running around outside your tank."

"My name is Ethel and I am looking for a new place to live. What's your name?" she replied, trying to be brave but feeling a little sick in her tummy.

"I'm Maxie, and you are taking a really big chance out here without Kevin and Timmy keeping an eye on you. You don't know if I would want to eat you or not, do you?" she said as she licked her paw.

"Are you going to eat me?" asked Ethel as she slowly started backing up, trying to look behind her but keeping her eyes on the cat.

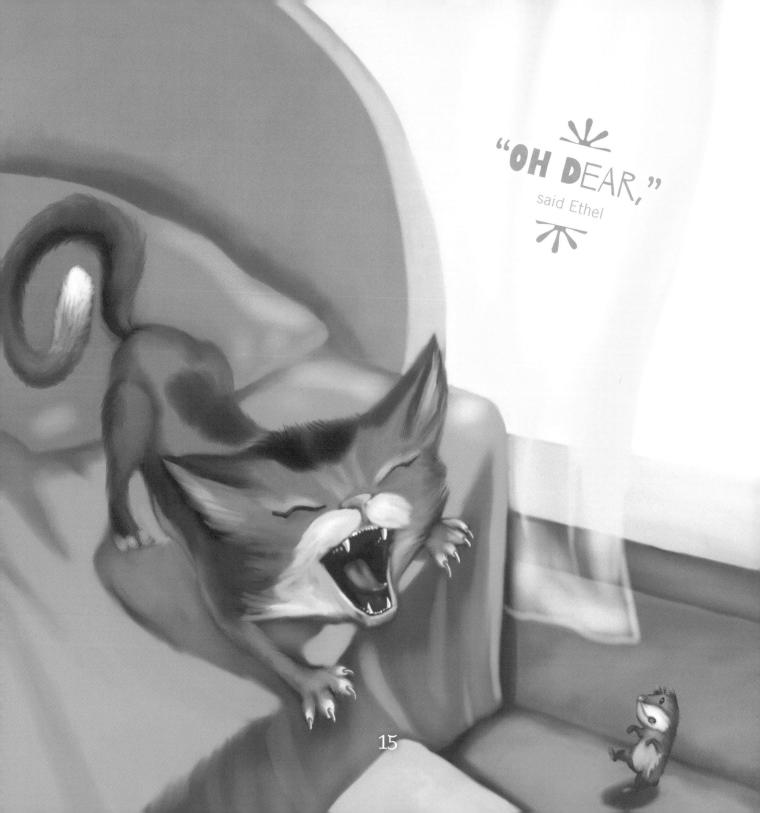

Maxie jumped down from the windowsill and walked to the edge of the bed. She looked down at Ethel and yawned. Ethel became very nervous as she stared inside the very large mouth with its big white fangs.

"No, I've already eaten," Maxie said as she stretched and laid down. "And right now it is time for my nap."

Ethel was too frightened by the size of Maxie's mouth to believe she wouldn't eat her so she continued to back up. When she was far enough away, she ran as fast as she could go.

Ethel ran until she found herself in the bathroom. "I need a place to hide until Maxie falls asleep," Ethel said to herself.

Ethel looked around and saw a big glass shower stall. "I know," she said. "I will hide in there."

Ethel climbed the floorboard on the wall to the shower ledge and fell in. It was slippery, wet and cold.

"Oh dear," said Ethel. "I don't like this at all. How am I going to get out of here? I'm stuck!"

Ethel sat down in the corner of the shower feeling sad. She had no place to go. She was all alone and all her food was gone; she had forgotten it under the dresser in the boy's room.

"I wish I was at home with my brothers and sisters," Ethel said. "Now I know for sure this wasn't such a good idea."

Ethel grew sadder and sadder as she sat and sat thinking about her brothers and sisters. Waiting and hoping that Kevin or Timmy would find her before Maxie did.

After a very long time, the light came on in the bathroom and there was Kevin standing in the doorway. Ethel peeked out from her corner and looked up at Kevin.

"Here I am, Kevin!" she thought to herself. "Please see me!"

"There you are Ethel! Kevin turned to the doorway and called for his brother. "Timmy! I found Ethel!" Timmy came running in.

"HERE I AM, KEVIN!" Ethel thought to herself.

Kevin, Timmy and Maxie who had been awakened by all the noise peered in the shower at Ethel; she was soaking wet.

"How did Ethel get all the way in here?" asked Timmy.

"We'll never know." Said Kevin with a smile. "Let's get her out of here and back to her brothers and sisters."

"Can I carry her?" Timmy asked. He bent down and scooped Ethel up into his hands. "Ethel, don't ever run away from home again!"

"I won't," thought Ethel, now sitting happily in his hand. "I just want to see my brothers and sisters again. I really missed them."

"I have a surprise for you," said Kevin as the four of them entered the bedroom. "Mom, Timmy and I went to the pet store and got you and your brothers and sisters a new home. It is much bigger and has lots of places to run."

"Wow!" thought Ethel, looking at her new home. There were now two tanks connected by a bright green tube sitting on the floor. There was a food dish and water bottle, as well as several running wheels, and sleeping huts in each tank.

20

"I'm home everyone!" Ethel cried as Timmy gently placed her into her new home. "I missed you all so much."

"Look Ethel," said Sadie. "This new home is great! Look at all the sleeping huts, you can have your own room!"

"That's okay," said Ethel. "I don't mind if I have to wait or share. I'll never run away from home again."

THE END

ABOUT THE AUTHOR

Kathy Rogo found her inspiration for *Ethel's New Home* from her two sons Kevin and TJ and a pet hamster named Ethel. This story is loosely based on Ethel's talent for escaping the hamster tank and then being found in the last places you would ever imagine. Kathy grew up in Woodland Hills, California and moved to Aspen, Colorado at age 23 and finally learned to ski three years after that. Kathy has a day job and writes in her spare time.

 **Friesen Press**

Suite 300 - 990 Fort St
Victoria, BC, Canada, V8V 3K2
www.friesenpress.com

ISBN
978-1-4602-5736-4 (Paperback)
978-1-4602-5737-1 (eBook)

1. Juvenile Fiction, Animals, Mice, Hamsters, Guinea Pigs, Etc.

Distributed to the trade by The Ingram Book Company

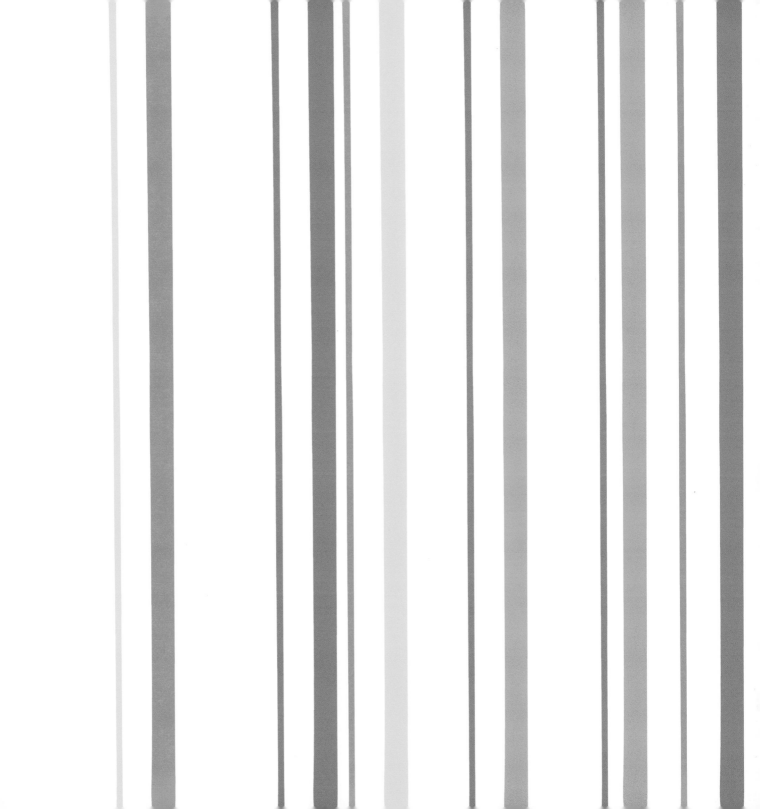

CPSIA information can be obtained at www.ICGtesting.com
Printed in the USA
LVIW01n2342030715
444961LV00003B/5

* 9 7 8 1 4 6 0 2 5 7 3 6 4 *